LIFE

written by Cynthia Rylant

illustrated by Brendan Wenzel

Beach Lane Books • New York   London   Toronto   Sydney   New Delhi

Life begins small.

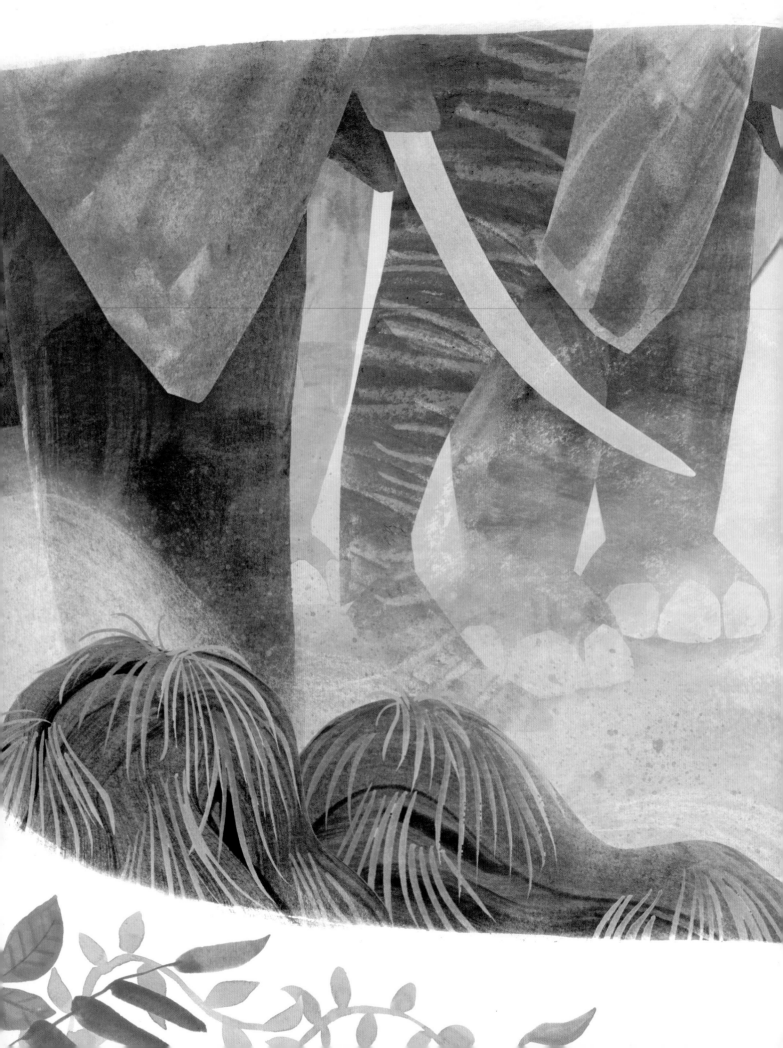

Even for the elephants.

Then it grows.

Beneath the Sun.

And the Moon.

Life grows.

Ask any animal on earth,
what do you love about life?

The hawk will say sky.

The camel will say sand.

The snake will say grasssssssssssss.

The turtle may remain quiet.
It has seen much in its hundred years.

But the turtle loves life. How could it not,
with so much rain on its back?

Life is not always easy.

There will probably be
a stretch of wilderness
now and then.

But wilderness eventually ends.

And there is always a new road to take.

Remember this:

in every corner of the world,
there is something to love.

And something

to protect.

And if, one day,
it seems nothing beautiful
will ever come your way again,

trust the rabbit
in the field

and the deer
who crosses your path.

Trust the wolf

and the wild geese
who find their way back home.

All these know something about life:

that everything is changing.

And it is worth
waking up in the morning
to see what might happen.

Because life begins small.

And grows.

For D. T. and D. H.
and all that grows around you—C. R.

For Caroline—B. W.

BEACH LANE BOOKS • An imprint of Simon & Schuster Children's Publishing Division • 1230 Avenue of the Americas, New York, New York 10020 • Text copyright © 2017 by Cynthia Rylant • Illustrations copyright © 2017 by Brendan Wenzel • All rights reserved, including the right of reproduction in whole or in part in any form. • BEACH LANE BOOKS is a trademark of Simon & Schuster, Inc. • For information about special discounts for bulk purchases, please contact Simon & Schuster Special Sales at 1-866-506-1949 or business@simonandschuster.com. • The Simon & Schuster Speakers Bureau can bring authors to your live event. For more information or to book an event, contact the Simon & Schuster Speakers Bureau at 1-866-248-3049 or visit our website at www.simonspeakers.com. • Book design by Lauren Rille
The text for this book was set in Adobe Garamond. • Manufactured in China
0417 SCP • First Edition
2 4 6 8 10 9 7 5 3 1
CIP data for this book is available from the Library of Congress.
ISBN 978-1-4814-5162-8 (hardcover)
ISBN 978-1-4814-5163-5 (eBook)

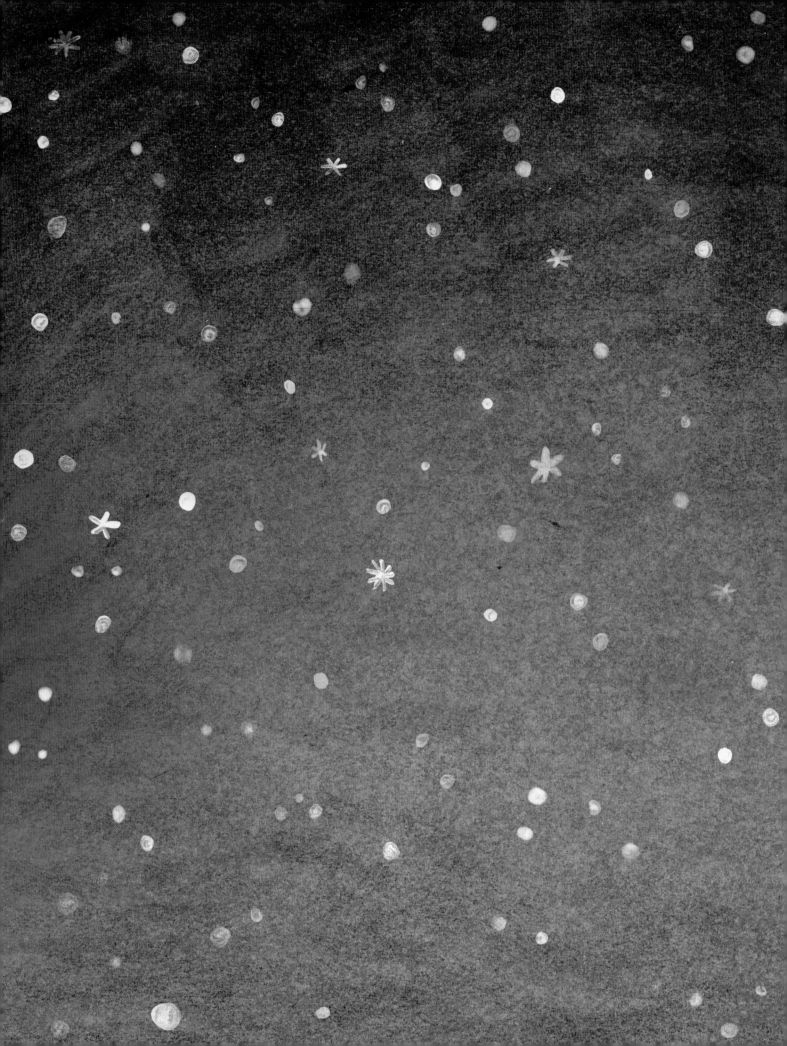